The Spirit of Giving

Seven Contemporary Christmas Tales

Ron Blicq

First published in Canada in 2012 by
R-G Productions, 569 Oxford St, Winnipeg MB R3M 3J2
(R-G Productions previously published as RGI International)

First Edition – September 2012

ISBN
978-1-4602-0196-1 (Hardcover)
978-1-4602-0197-8 (Paperback)
978-1-4602-0198-5 (eBook)

Although most of the stories in The Spirit of Giving are based on real events, the names of people and their locations have been changed to protect their privacy.

Produced by:

FriesenPress
Suite 300 – 852 Fort Street
Victoria, BC, Canada V8W 1H8

www.friesenpress.com

Distributed to the trade by The Ingram Book Company

The Spirit of Giving is also available as an ebook.

Table of Contents

Other Works by Ron Blicq

Novels/Biography

Choosing Home
Au Revoir, Sarnia Chérie
(Good-bye, Dear Guernsey)
You Will Write, Won't You?

Theatre

Closure
Shades of Grey
The Railway Children
Chords, Accords and Discords
Five Children and a Psammead
The Popsicle-Stick Wand
The Sicilian Wine Test
Battle of the Wands
Sudoku Fever
Puss in Boots

Education
Books

On The Move
Get to the Point!
Technically-Write!
Administratively-Write!
Communicating at Work
Guidelines for Report Writing

Theatre

Have You Ever Tried Listening?
Flying Like Estelle
A Room for Two

Television

Go For It!
6 Around a Table
Sell Yourself Well
Scaling the Pyramid
So, You Have to Give a Talk?
Sharpening Your Communication Skills

The Spirit of Giving
Seven Contemporary Christmas Tales

Christmas Giving
isn't only about gifts
wrapped in brightly
coloured paper

Ron Blicq

About the Tales

You might ask: how could letters I have written to family and friends around the world possibly become a book of Christmas tales?

It wasn't planned, I can assure you; the idea just evolved, a step at a time.

In 1995 I decided I would no longer buy Christmas cards but would send a donation to ***Unicef*** equal to the amount I would have paid for the cards. Then, in place of the cards, each year I would write a personal letter as a Christmas Greeting and mail it early, to ensure it arrived *before* Christmas.

That was the first step, the easy one.

The second step was more difficult, because I had to decide what my Christmas letters should contain. About one thing I was certain: they would *not* become a dull, week-by-week description of what *I* had done over the past 12 months!

So each year, in the fall, I have searched for an event that I have either witnessed or heard of, which I could fashion into a story. These stories—there have been 16 so far, one per year—have become the key feature in my annual Christmas letters.

Then, last year, as a gift for my family, I assembled seven of the stories into a "Christmas Memoir." The family so liked the idea, they persuaded me to fashion the stories into this book.

First, you will meet Myles Reddish and his two daughters Debbie and Chris, who live in Winnipeg as I do, at the eastern end of the Canadian Prairies. You will read how they experienced Christmas when the girls were 15 and 12, and then in Chapter 5 you will meet them again, when the girls were in their mid-to-late teens, as they experienced a very different Christmas.

In Chapter 2 you will meet Keith who, because he and his wife Meghan live in England where they seldom see snow, decided to build a realistic snowman as a decoration for their front garden, only to discover their snowman had developed a life of its own.

In Chapter 3 you will hear the voices of children from around the world, who tell us what Christmas is like for them. The excerpts come from letters written by youngsters in Europe, Scandinavia, India, South Africa, New Zealand, the UK, Canada, and the US, with each casting a different light on how they experience Christmas. Surprisingly, they only rarely mention the physical gifts they receive, although many describe in detail the unique foods they enjoy.

The children's views are followed by a personal reminiscence of a Christmas Eve I experienced as a child, which has forever remained in my memory.

Two chapters are about people who were travelling to a special Christmas destination, only to have their plans disrupted in a way they had not foreseen. In Chapter 4 you will meet a visitor who flew in unexpectedly from the arctic and wrung significant changes to my friend Raymond Brouard's Christmas plans. And then in Chapter 6 you will meet 13- and 11-year-old Torrance and Jasmyn who, travelling alone, experienced a weather extreme that prevented them from celebrating Christmas in the special way their family and friends had planned for them.

I have chosen these particular stories because each tells about someone, or sometimes more than one person, who has contributed to what I call 'The Spirit of Giving.' They are based on real events, although in some cases I have changed a person's name and occasionally a location.

I hope you enjoy reading the stories, as much as I enjoyed writing them.

RSB
May 2012

1
Christmas Cookies

Although Myles Reddish and I have been friends for over 30 years, our paths cross only occasionally. So, when we do meet, we relish the opportunity to exchange information about each other and our families.

In April of 2006 we met unexpectedly at The Forks in Winnipeg, where his daughters Debbie and Chris were attending a play at Manitoba Theatre for Young People. As its name suggests, The Forks is situated at the point where the Assiniboine and the Red Rivers meet. Historically, it was a meeting place for First Nations' people, then it became a settlement beside a Hudson Bay fort known as Upper Fort Garry, and eventually the site of the railway station and locomotive repair sheds of the Canadian National Railway. The repair sheds and surrounding area have now been fashioned into a very successful meeting place that embraces a shopping centre, theatre, children's museum, hotel, numerous ethnic eating places and—currently under construction—the Canadian Museum for Human Rights.

But first let me tell you more about Myles. We met originally at Red River College in 1981, where he appeared in a class of students studying electrical engineering technology I was teaching. From his records I knew that after leaving high school in Minnedosa, a provincial town some 200 kilometres west of Winnipeg, he had worked in his family's printing business for eight years. Then, preferring to strike out on his own, he headed into the city so he could obtain a diploma that would make him eligible to apply to Manitoba Hydro, the province's power utility and a major employer of technical graduates. As the months advanced and I learned still more about my students, I discovered I had known Myles's father when we had both served in the Royal Canadian Air Force many years earlier. From that moment a casual and comfortable friendship grew between us.

We touched base occasionally after Myles graduated and obtained the job he wanted, partly through an engineering society we both belonged to, and sometimes just by happenstance. Through a mutual friend I heard he had married and was living in a small town near the city, and in time I heard he had two daughters, about two years apart.

Ten years ago we happened to meet in a shopping mall where I was doing my Christmas shopping. He told me he had just been through a difficult divorce and was delighted that the court had ruled that his daughters were to live with him (they were then about 8 and 5). It had been an expensive experience, he said, and ruefully dug his hand into his pocket.

"Would you believe this is my net worth until I get paid at the end of the week?" Myles held out his hand, palm up, with a dime, a nickel, and two pennies resting on it.

He grinned: "Seventeen cents is so much better than twenty-five cents. A quarter would be lonely and just flop around in my pocket; I'd hardly know it was there. But seventeen cents: you can feel the coins are there and hear them jingle as they rub against each other. You know you've got something,"

I remember thinking that Christmas would be slim for his daughters Debbie and Chris that year, but with Myles's positive approach I sensed they would be alright. And that memory was re-enforced when we met at The Forks seven years later.

"Could you believe that Debbie has just turned 16, and Chris is 13," he said as we climbed the eight steps leading up to the Johnston Terminal, now a shopping plaza with a long coffee shop like a gallery with tall windows looking out onto the railway station and the bridges over the two rivers.

With steaming mugs of hot chocolate in our hands, we settled into two wire-backed chairs one on each side of a small table against a window. I was facing southwest, from where I could see the curve of the Assiniboine River, with leafless trees on the opposite bank leaning gauntly over the gently flowing water. From the opposite side of the table Myles was watching a freight train with three locomotives at the front, as it chugged ponderously from the east and passed along a track that runs beside the passenger station.

As we compared notes about our families, Myles told me an anecdote about his elder daughter. "Christmas was a little different last December," he said, a little ruefully I thought.

"Different?" I echoed, leaving the door open for him to continue if he chose to. I didn't want him to feel I was pushing him into describing something personal about himself and his daughters.

"It's just that Debbie is growing up, and I haven't been using my eyes."

Myles took a sip of his hot chocolate—thoughtfully, as

though he was reminiscing privately—then launched, at first a little uneasily, into a tale that, as the minutes passed, I began to realise had the makings of a 21st-century Christmas fable; a modern fable yet one with a Dickensian touch to it.

So here it is, just as Myles told it to me.

~~~

Christmas is pretty traditional for Debbie, Chris and me. We have found a pattern we like and we tend to stick to it. Some people might think it's boring, always the same routine, but for the girls it sort-of sharpens their anticipation, makes them that much more aware.

We didn't plan it or do it intentionally; it just grew over the years. And for the girls, having only one parent—well, at least only the one parent they ever see—I feel that keeping tradition is important, like a security blanket.

That's why it came as a surprise to find that Debbie wanted to do something different. No, that's not quite true: she didn't say she wanted to do it; she just stepped in and did it. Pulled a rug right out from under me, and reminded me that I had to recognize that now she was almost 16 I must step back, avoid being over-protective, and allow her to do more things—make decisions for herself.

Christmas Eve we always drive to my sister's, in Minnedosa. She and Stephen have two boys a couple of years younger than my girls, and somehow they seem to get on well. Maybe it's because they see each other only once or twice a year, Minnedosa being a two-and-a-half-hour drive from the city. Val always wants us to stay overnight and into Christmas Day,
~~~

but I resist, knowing the girls like being in their own home for "The Tree" on Christmas morning..

So every year Val sets up a mid-afternoon lunch/ dinner—always roast beef with Yorkshire pudding and roast potatoes—so we can set off for the return journey shortly after 7 and be in our own home by 9:30. After the dinner we play charades—Chris is the sharp one at guessing the words—and watch a couple of Christmas videos, like *Christmas in Old St. Peters* and *The Grinch Who Stole Christmas* – always the same ones, but no one seems to tire of them.

That day sets a nice start to our Christmas—a "family" day—and as we drive home I can almost sense the girls' contentment. (Next Christmas, Debbie insists, she is going to do the driving, so I can have a drink or two with my meal.)

The days when the girls would waken at 5 a.m. on Christmas morning are over, thank goodness. Now it's more like 8 a.m., and I appreciate that. Even then, it's always Debbie who clumps down the stairs first, turns on the tree lights, shakes the parcels noisily, and puts on a Christmas CD good and loud to make sure Chris and I hear her and get up. She's the one who's always eager to start the ritual unwrapping, and the loudest one with the "oohs" and "ahs" as each gift is revealed.

So when I came down on Christmas morning I was surprised to find Chris was there first. Still wrapped in her voluminous dressing gown, she had put the music on loud and got the coffee perking (for me) and had three mince tarts warming in the oven—all the things that her older sister normally did.

Debbie has certainly become a bit jaded, I thought. She has never slept in this late on Christmas Day!

When the Little Ben on the mantelpiece chimed twice, signalling 8:30, Chris looked up with a pensive: "Can't we start?"

"Go and get her up," I said. "It's time she was down here."

Chris scrambled up the stairs, opened Debbie's bedroom door, and called out: "Deb?"

There was a moment's pause, then I could hear her footsteps crossing the floor to the bathroom. She threw open that door.

"Deb?" she called, louder this time. There was no answer.

I was already climbing the stairs. "She's not here?" This was unbelievable, unlocking all my fears.

Chris shook her head.

"Do you know where she is?"

Another shake of the head. Chris is so genuine, so honest, I knew she wasn't covering for her sister.

I didn't know whether to be scared for Debbie, or just angry with her for not saying she was going somewhere. The fear took over even more when I pushed her door open and saw that her bed was a scrambled mess, the duvet and pillows hanging lopsidedly over one side.

So at least she had slept here. But could someone have broken in and abducted her?

I checked the windows, but they were secure.

I looked on the bedside table for a note, but there was none. And none in the kitchen or living room either.

"You're sure you don't know where she is?" I demanded, quite unnecessarily, for I could see tears welling up in Chris's eyes.

I strode over to the bay window, pulled the curtains apart, and looked to see if she had taken the car (on her beginners' license? – oh, lord!). But no, it stood there, covered in about seven centimetres of snow. There were traces of wheel tracks, where a vehicle had pulled up behind it and then backed out, but they were almost filled in with the snow that was still falling. Now, that did worry me.

I was already reaching for the phone—not sure whether I should call some of her friends' parents, or even the police—but Chris rested a hand on mine.

"No, don't, Dad" she said. She shook her head, looked earnestly up at me. "Give her time." I gave her a questioning look. "Until…" she hesitated… "nine o'clock."

Twenty minutes.

I paced, going from one window to another. This is no way to start our Christmas Day, I thought.

At five minutes before nine I saw her boyfriend's parents' Volkswagen pull into our driveway. Through the windshield I could see Debbie lean across and give him a kiss. Then she flung open her door and leapt out. As he started to back down the drive she gave him a quick wave and then ran toward our back door, her scarf trailing behind her in the breeze.

"Where the hell have you been?" I bellowed, before she had even closed the door.

(I had resolved to be calm, to let her explain, but relief from the fear I had felt was pushing me.)

"Starting Christmas!" she said. And she laughed.

"It was great."

"With William?"

"He helped me." She pulled off her coat and scarf. "You know all those Christmas cookies I baked?"

"Y-e-s..."

"They weren't for us."

"They were for William?"

"No, no. He was helping me. He made the drinks: ginger cordial. I made the cookies."

"For what? For whom?"

"For people who have to work on Christmas Eve and into Christmas morning."

Debbie said she and William had given a small bottle of hot ginger cordial and a bag of Christmas cookies to everyone they could find at places like the gas bar, the donut shop, the nursing home, and even the community police office.

"Why didn't you tell me?" I asked, relief clear in my voice, although still coloured a bit by my annoyance. "So I'd know where you were. Chris and I wouldn't have been so worried!"

"Because you would've wanted to help. Always you do. You would have insisted."

Yes, well ... I guess she was right about that.

"I didn't even tell Chris." She held a hand out to her sister. "Sorry, Chris, but I wanted it to be something I did on my own. My own idea. And William said he'd drive me. He helped, too."

She laughed. "He didn't tell his parents, either. And the same sort of thing's probably happening in his house."

"Not any more, not here," I said, and pulled her toward me, gave her a hug. "Merry Christmas, my dear."

Later, after the ritual opening of presents and we were sitting over bacon and eggs, which Debbie insisted she would cook this year (and I said "OK", and she did a fantastic job), I asked what sort of reaction she got from the people she had visited.

"Oh, it was so different. Some people said they were surprised and so happy that we should even think of doing it. Some asked how come no one had thought of doing it before. Would you believe there was a really bitchy old guy in the gas bar who just pushed us aside and asked what the catch was; what we thought we were up to. He wouldn't even listen when we tried to explain." She gulped. "But, you know, the hardest to take—for me—was the old lady who sits inside the door of the old people's home on Wellington, like a night clerk. She just burst into tears. Almost made me cry too."

~~~

Through the coffee shop window at The Forks I could see two teen-age girls walking around the edge of the skating pond, clearly looking for someone. *Debbie and Chris*, I thought, and pointed them out to Myles. He nodded, tapped on the glass, and they turned. Big grins, and they ran up the steps and into the coffee bar.

Introductions, followed by another round of hot chocolate.

While I was at the counter, with Chris beside me (she had volunteered to help carry the drinks), I heard Debbie say, a tiny bit of concern in her voice: "You all right, Dad?"

"Sure," he said. "Of course."

I glanced around and could see her standing behind him running a hand through his hair, with her other hand resting
~~~

on his shoulder. Myles was grinning like a Cheshire cat.

Yes, I thought, warmed by the depth of Debbie's feeling for her father, *Myles is doing a great job with his daughters. They're just fine. All three of them.*

2

Keith's Snowman

My friend Keith, who lives in the village of Oakenhurst, 20 kilometres west of Oxford in England, retired five years ago. We both came from the Canadian Prairies, and both had become navigators, first in the RCAF and subsequently in the Royal Air Force. We met originally at Changi airport in Singapore, when I used to night-stop there en route between Australia and England, and later when we were both based at Shawbury, an advanced navigation training school in Shropshire.

Three years later, when we had completed our terms of service with the Air Force, I returned to Canada. By then Keith had married Meghan—an English lass—and chose to stay in England, working in a newsagents shop owned by Meghan's father in Banbury, some 25 kilometres north of Oxford. We have kept in touch over the years, initially by email and now by Skype.

Keith eventually took over the newsagents shop, which he and Meghan ran together until they decided to retire.

Then when they sold the shop they bought a Cotswold-stone cottage in Oakenhurst.

After a month or two, however, Keith found time was beginning to hang heavily on his hands: he's a guy who likes to keep busy, and Meghan likes it that way.

"Otherwise," she confided to me on my most recent visit, "he always seems to be underfoot."

So Keith decided to build an extension onto his garage and create a handy workshop equipped with a workbench and a jigsaw and an assortment of cutting and shaving tools. Onto the wall he screwed pegboard so his tools could hang in neat rows.

"It's finished," Keith announced to Meghan as they sat at the kitchen table having their elevenses (for my North American friends, that's morning coffee-break in England, traditionally held about 10:30).

Meghan brushed a lock of hair away from her forehead and tucked it under the scarf she binds around her head whenever she's cleaning house. "So, what are you going to make?"

"I'd like to make something for *you*, for the house." He felt that was a suitable answer, since he had spent so much time (and cash) building the workshop.

Meghan stalled, doubtful about his handiwork. She hesitated because she didn't want what might turn out to be only partly presentable to end up littering (which was the exact word she chose to use, although not to Keith) the nicely furnished home she was so proud of.

It was October by then, which prompted her to venture an unusual idea: "What about making a man-size Christmas decoration, like a Father Christmas with coloured lights? You've always admired what other people put up each year, to entertain children passing their houses."

(Here, I should also explain that in Britain “Santa Claus” is generally called “Father Christmas.” And merrymakers, instead of saying “Merry Christmas” greet each other by saying “Happy Christmas”.)

Keith thought her suggestion was brilliant and the next day started drawing up a fully-dimensioned plan on squared paper.

“I’m going to make a snowman,” he announced when he came in for that morning’s elevenses. “No one has done that, and you can only rarely make a real snowman here: we just don’t get enough snow.”

It took him six weeks.

Keith constructed a light but sturdy wooden frame over which he fastened sheets of pliable white Styrofoam. In a second-hand shop he found an old pair of army boots to serve as feet, and a Scots military beret which he perched at a jaunty angle on its head. He glued large black buttons down its front and even fashioned a grey tweed breast pocket with a red hankie poking out. He used two bright blue marbles for its eyes, an orange-painted wooden clothes peg for its nose, and a mouth with teeth he picked up in a magician’s shop in Witney. It stood 5½ feet high (about 1.7 metres).

Meghan was impressed when Keith led her out to his workshop in early December. “That’s a real work of art,” she said and placed a hand on the snowman’s shoulder. “The children are going to love it.”

And then she added: “So, what are you going to call him? It is a ‘he’, isn’t it?”

“Have you ever heard of a female snow-*man*?” Keith snorted. They both laughed.

Meghan shivered: it was cold in the workshop. “Come in for elevenses,” she said, “I have made the coffee.”

As they sat across from each other at the small deal table in their kitchenette, Meghan suggested names for Keith's creation. She started with 'Harvey,' then 'Edward,' and finally 'Roland.' But each time Keith demurred.

"No," he said, pushing his coffee cup across the table, toward Meghan, which she knew meant he wanted half a cup more (always one-and-a-half cups for Keith, never two full cups; he was adamant about that).

"The snowman is special" he explained. "He needs a name that has *character*."

"Right." Meghan pushed the half-filled cup and the sugar bowl toward Keith. "Then, what about 'Morgan'?"

"Uh-uh… sounds too Welsh."

"Stuart?" Meghan was teasing really. Anticipating his answer, she added: "Too much like a Scot?"

"Morgan was closer."

Keith swung around in his chair, grasped a pencil and paper from the sideboard, and started penciling in names. But each time he shook his head and drew a horizontal line through the name. Then, on the eighth attempt, he grinned: "Yes… that's it!"

Meghan lifted her reading glasses, which were dangling from a black string around her neck. "Very nice, dear: 'Marvin.' I like that."

Keith's grin widened. He nodded, pulled on his Wellington boots, and asked if he could borrow Meghan's sewing basket. That afternoon he stitched **Marvin** in bold, red script letters across the snowman's pocket,

The following morning—it was December 10th —Keith carried Marvin out onto the front lawn and stood his feet on a sturdy board with indentations carved in it, so Marvin wouldn't blow over. Then he erected three white spotlights, two pointing upward toward Marvin from the front corners of the lawn and one pointing downward from a wooden triangular structure he had mounted on the cottage roof.

Reaction from the townspeople was far greater than either Keith or Meghan had expected. Each evening they sat in their front window, with the interior lights off so they could not be seen, and watched dozens of families walk or drive up to see Keith's handiwork. A week later, Marvin gained some notoriety, as did Keith and Meghan, when a reporter and photographer arrived to make a feature story for the Oxford Mail. Marvin's picture appeared on page 3 on December 22nd, with Keith and Meghan standing one on each side. (Meghan has since admitted to me that she was wrong to doubt Keith's workshop capability.)

But Keith's Christmas pleasure was destroyed on Boxing Day (December 26th). When he pulled back the bedroom curtains and looked out of the window, he saw that Marvin had disappeared! In his place stood a three-foot post with a triangular red flag on its top.

Keith slowly, sadly, pulled on his Wellington boots and strode out to the garden. An envelope had been stapled onto the post, with Keith's name on it. Tearing it open, Keith found a copy of the Oxford Mail article and photo, but also a postcard of Father Christmas on his sleigh with eight reindeer pulling him away over the rooftops. When he turned the postcard over, he could see a handwritten note, penned in blue ink:

> *Dear Keith*
>
> *Father Christmas has invited me to travel with him to the north pole, so please forgive me if I am away for a while. I promise: I will come back, because I know I will miss you and Meghan.*

Love, Marvin

Then, squeezed in at the foot of the card, Marvin had apparently hastily inserted a postscript, written with a stubby pencil:

> *P.S. This is a great opportunity*
> *for me to see a real snowman,*
> *made of the real stuff.*

To make Keith feel even sadder, when he walked back into the house to tell Meghan of the disaster, the telephone was ringing. It was the reporter from the Oxford Mail, calling to thank him for a great story.

"Not so great now," Keith grunted, and told the reporter about Marvin and the note.

"I'll be right there!" the reporter shouted, and 30 minutes later his car screeched to a stop in front of the house. And that was how Marvin's note got to be photo-copied and appear on the front page of the Oxford Mail on New Year's Eve.

But that was no solace for Keith who, to Meghan's annoyance, padlocked the door of his new workshop and sat day after day in the front room, staring out of the window and sipping cups of tea.

Keith moped for six weeks, until mid-February, when a postcard dropped through their mailbox and plopped onto the 'Welcome' mat inside the front door.

Meghan saw it first and shouted to Keith: "There's a card from Marvin! Come and see."

They peered at it together. The front of the card showed a photograph of a polar bear standing in deep snow, and the words *Churchill, Manitoba* printed in bold letters across the top. On the other side was a handwritten note.

Hello, Keith:

I had a cool time with Father Christmas, but found all those noisy green elves running around disturbed my peace of mind. So now I am heading south.

In another way I was happy to be in Churchill, because I found that polar bears are as white as I am!

I will write again soon.

Marvin

"It's a trick." Meghan was critical. "Someone around here is pulling your leg."

Keith looked at the right-hand top corner of the postcard. "I don't think so. It has a Canadian stamp and if you look carefully you can see the postmark has *Churchill* on it and the date: 5th February."

Keith decided not to tell anyone—and least of all the reporter from the Oxford Mail. "People will start thinking I made it up, just for a laugh."

Meghan agreed, and went back to putting up with Keith moping around the house. But a little less, really, because he re-opened his workshop and spent some time puttering around out there.

In late April Keith received another postcard, but this time from the opposite end of the world: New Zealand! On the front was a photograph of Marvin, and he was standing next to a policeman, who had one arm resting on Marvin's shoulder. Keith turned the card over:

No, I am not being arrested, Keith! Tell Meghan that this friendly police-man directed me to a cool Bed and Breakfast in Christchurch, which is a pretty city in New Zealand's south island, where I am studying the scenery for a while.

It's autumn here and the leaves are falling off the trees. Soon there will be snow and I will like it even better then.

Love, Marvin.

A third postcard arrived in September, bearing a postage stamp from India. This time there was a photograph of Marvin talking earnestly to a woman wearing a brightly coloured sari and a maroon headscarf, with them both standing beneath a sign that read:

Arrivals, Dum Dum Airport, Calcutta.

On the other side, Keith recognized Marvin's now familiar handwriting:

My greetings to Keith and Meghan:

Whew. It is hot here. This time I am glad I'm not a real snowman, for I would last no longer than 10 minutes! I'd be just a puddle on the floor. It almost makes me wish I was back in Oxfordshire...

But not yet.

Your friend,

Marvin

Keith, rather than being despondent, was elated by the words "not yet." *So Marvin is coming back*, he thought, and trudged out to his workshop. He realized that he had begun to look forward to receiving the cards and had almost given up wondering how this could all be happening.

But not Meghan: she remained suspicious that someone local was writing the cards or arranging with someone in each location that Marvin 'visited' to write and mail a card. She feared that one day someone they knew would appear on their doorstep and chortle over the trick he had played. *That's funny*, Meghan thought, *I never think the person doing this might be a woman!*

That evening, as Keith and Meghan dined on a crab salad she had made for their supper, Keith announced: "For next Christmas I'm going to build a thatched country house with little lights in the windows. Nothing with legs, so it can't walk away."

Meghan nodded in agreement, but with a nagging question still in her mind: *Does Keith think all this is real? Surely he knows it's only someone playing a trick on him?*

But, even if it was a trick, she still wondered how it was being done.

It took nearly three months for Keith to finish the new Christmas display and when he set it up on their front lawn everyone agreed it was wonderful. He had built a 5-foot-high old-fashioned country home, with a barn beside it, and had painted both so they looked as though they had been built with Cotswold stone. Each was topped with a thatched roof (which Keith had made from rushes he had gathered from a marsh near South Cerney). The doors and window frames he had painted a bright blue, which stood out clearly beside the sand-coloured walls and grey roofs.

But it was at night that the whole display really glowed, for every window had little lights inside it. Keith had secured the house and barn onto a solid platform he had built on the front edge of the lawn, so that people walking by could peer in the windows and see carved figures sitting around a dining table with Christmas fare set on it, and even a brightly-coloured miniature Christmas cracker in front of each person. A child was holding her cracker up, inviting the boy on her left to pull it with her. And behind the family stood a room-height miniature Christmas tree strung with tiny lights.

At the top end of the table, a be-whiskered white-haired man stood brandishing a large knife and fork, ready to carve a tiny turkey sitting in an oval dish in front of him.

Keith's display became the talk not only of Oakenhurst but also of nearby villages and larger towns, drawing visitors from as far away as Cirencester and Cheltenham.

Meghan was so proud of her husband and even murmured to herself that maybe it would be all right for Keith to make something for their home. Yet there was an unexpected twist to Keith's success: now Meghan found that visiting the local shops had become a chore, for she was constantly being stopped by local townspeople who wanted to talk about Marvin's disappearance as well as the new display house.

Just one week before Christmas still another postcard arrived. This time it was from Marseilles in the south of France. The photograph showed Marvin (whose mouth now seemed to have a wicked grin!) standing on a beach with waves breaking on the shore behind him and a bathing beauty on each side with an arm around his waist. (*Waist? Does a snowman really have a waist?* Keith wondered.*)*

This time the message contained only eleven words:

> *My journey is sort-of delayed;*
> *I like the scenery here.*

Meghan, who was peering over Keith's shoulder, wagged a finger in front of the photograph. "Don't you dare show that to anyone; those young women are only half-dressed!"

As the next seven days rolled around, more and more

people came to see Keith's contribution to the Christmas scene, particularly in the early evening, before children were tucked into their beds. For the first time the village of Oakenhurst experienced traffic jams, but the three local police officers were instructed by the mayor to be tolerant because Keith's display had done so much to promote the village within the Oxfordshire community.

As Christmas Eve lengthened into Christmas night, and Keith and Meghan prepared for bed, he opened the bedroom window and listened.

"Yep," he whispered to Meghan. "I can hear them: sleigh bells, right up there, above the rooftops."

Meghan nodded. "Yes, dear, you're right." But she also shook her head, wondering at her husband's tricky imagination. At the same time she was well pleased with him—no, proud would be a better word—for creating so much happiness with his new-found hobby. The hundreds of children who had peered into the windows of the little house clearly were delighted: every evening she and Keith had sat in their living room and listened happily to the children's "Oohs" and "Aahs."

But it was a very different sound that awakened Keith the next morning. *Oh, no*, he thought as he jumped out of bed, *someone's stolen my Christmas scene!*

Yet, when he pulled back the bedroom curtains he saw that the cottage and barn were still intact, but a large crowd of men, women and children were already standing in front of the garden, laughing and pointing toward it.

For there, standing beside the house, almost like he was looking down the miniature chimney pots, stood *Marvin!* Keith rushed downstairs, quickly followed by Meghan, and pushed open the front door, walking barefoot across the dew-covered lawn.

Marvin looked clean and white, just as he had exactly one year before. The only difference was a note pinned to his pocket, with just four words penned onto it:

Push my top button.

The crowd behind Keith and Meghan had grown strangely still, as they watched Keith lean hesitantly forward with a tremulous finger pointing at Marvin, just below his toothy smile.

"Do it!" Meghan whispered into his ear.

Keith pushed the button, but just gently. Nothing happened.

Meghan placed a hand on his elbow and urged him to push harder. The greater pressure caused a gravelly voice to erupt from inside Marvin's body:

"Hello, Keith; hello, Meghan."

The crowd was silent now, leaning forward to catch every word:

> *"May I say Happy Christmas to you and all your friends. I'm home for good now and will be glad that I don't have to travel any more."*

There were tears in both Keith's and Meghan's eyes as the crowd behind them started chanting:

"Happy Christmas, Marvin; Happy Christmas, Marvin…!"

XMAS

3

Children's Views of Christmas

For the year 2000—to mark the start of the new millennium—I asked children from around the world to write me a short piece describing how they celebrate Christmas where they live, and to tell me what they particularly like about the Christmas season.

The idea was prompted by a radio program that the Canadian Broadcasting Corporation beams to its listeners nonstop from nine in the morning to seven in the evening on the Sunday immediately before Christmas. The CBC collaborates with broadcasting companies from countries around the world, particularly from Europe, with each presenting close to an hour of music and singing by well-known orchestras and choirs in their particular land. I choose it as the day on which I wrap Christmas gifts, do some pre-Christmas baking, and simply relax as the music and voices swell into my home.

The children who responded to my request ranged from 8 to 14 years of age. Here is how they described their

Christmas, with many of them writing far more eloquently than I might have done at their age.

I'm going to start with Adele, who lives on the Island of Guernsey in the English Channel, which is a British island nestled close to the coast of France. She wrote:

> *I love Christmas because it is a special time for everyone, and everyone is equally happy. I actually enjoy Christmas more than my Birthday, because although it is fun being in the centre of attention on your birthday, it's even better if you get to share the fun with everybody, especially your loved ones.*
>
> *Everyone goes to bed that night with smiles on their faces.*

Now lets travel north, to Norway, with thoughts drawn from a letter written by Tuva:

> *On Christmas Eve, in the morning, I watch the film "3 Nuts for Cinderella" on television. In it, Cinderella gets a ball gown, a wedding dress, and a hunter's outfit. Afterward we eat rice pudding with just one almond in it, and the one who finds the almond in their dish wins a marzipan pig.*
>
> *In the evening we eat pork ribs and sausages for our Christmas dinner. I don't like the ribs very much, except for the crackling.*
>
> *I wake up early on Christmas Day. I get up very quietly while the others are still asleep and watch television, play with my Christmas toys, and eat sweets. I have a Christmas pixie hat that I wear all the time, even indoors!*

If it has snowed, I like to go outside and build snow lanterns and snowmen with my friends. Sometimes we can see the Northern Lights in the evening. The light waves like a flag across the dark sky, often in many different colours: white, purple and green mixed with yellow or orange.

Tuva's mother included a note with Tuva's letter, in which she explained that most of the time Tuva lives with her in Oslo, but part of the year she journeys 560 kilometres north, to Trondheim, to spend time with her father.

On the other side of the world—far, far, south—here's Sam, who lives in Christchurch, on New Zealand's South Island:

On Christmas Day, as it is usually hot, Dad cooks Christmas lunch on the barbecue, and our grandparents, aunts and uncles spend the day with us.

We sit outside on the large veranda around a table under a wide umbrella. For lunch we have salmon and steak with salads, and for dessert we have ice cream, strawberries, trifle and Pavlova.

Then after lunch we take the boat to the lake and go water-skiing and swimming.

Back to Europe now and to Tarik, who is 9 and lives in Berlin, Germany. At the top of his letter, his mother Marlies wrote: *Tarik can't write much in English yet, so I asked him to tell me about Christmas and these were his words*:

To me, the days before Christmas are special because we have a pretty decorated apartment. Mummy is baking cookies and Christmas cakes and already it smells like Christmas.

We celebrate Christmas on the 24th of December. In the afternoon we decorate our Christmas tree and put up a nativity scene. Then I have to wait in my room until the early evening, which seems to take such a long time, while presents and a plate full of sweets and cookies are arranged around the tree. Then my parents call me into the living room and we wish each other Merry Christmas and sing some Christmas songs together. Then, at last, we open the presents, which is followed by a special dinner.

If we spend Christmas at my grandmother's big house near the mountains, we usually get snow and go for long walks or toboggan down the hills.

Marlies explained that Tarik's father comes from the Barbados and that Tarik also talked about that:

My father has told me that his family sprinkles sand around the house to make it look like snow. The evening before the 25th they bake sweet bread, which they eat with baked ham and macaroni pie, rice and peas.

In the Barbados, they love to listen to music, specially Christmas music.

It's interesting how many of these young people remember so clearly what they *eat* at Christmas! But not Rebecca, who comes from Yorkshire in England:

To me, the best thing about Christmas is going to my parents' ward for their Christmas party (my parents are both nurses). They work with elderly people who can't look after themselves any more. Every year, 'Father Christmas' visits to give them presents. Just to see their old, fragile faces smile when they are given a present is such a great pleasure.

Now over to Georgianna, who is age 12 and lives in Mumbai, India, where she is in Class V at the Bombay Scottish School. She says she likes to be called 'Georgy':

India is a country with many religions, and we Christians are a minority in this country. Christmas is celebrated in a big way in places like Goa and Kerala, where there are a large number of Christians. In the other states, Christmas is a time of celebrating the birth of Christ for the Christians, while for the others it is a time for entertaining their children with the gifts and goodies that Santa Claus has to offer.

In India, Christmas is looked upon as a peaceful and pleasant festival celebrated by a peace-loving community; in that way it is unlike some of the noisy festivals that occur. Midnight masses, carol services, Christmas parties, family gatherings, and exchanging sweets and cakes form the highlights of the festival. Schools and colleges close down for ten days, for Christmas vacations. Carols add a special touch to the season, floating down from the open windows of homes decorated with bright lights and stars of all colours and sizes.

Christmas time is the busiest time of the year for me. No sooner than my exams are over in December, I get busy with Christmas concert practices in school and at church. I get so busy that I hardly get time to go out with my mum to choose my Christmas dress or gifts!

The most exciting part about the season is decorating our 6-foot Christmas tree. My mischievous little sister and my little dog play an important role in decorating the tree.

Our Christmas tree forms the major attraction for all our non-Christian friends in the neighbourhood. My mother makes a lot of sweets and cakes which we proudly distribute to all our neighbours. We children even have a Christmas party for all our little friends, where we get together ahead of time and prepare our own sweets and eats.

Late on Christmas Day, after all the parties and fun have ended, my mother draws us together and reminds us of the importance of Christmas, its history, and the special message it has for all of us kids.

I received four short comments from children in Canada, which is my home as well as theirs. Let's start with 11-year-old Graham, in Winnipeg:

I like Christmas because the whole time and place are wonderful. When there's not much snow—which doesn't happen often in Winnipeg in December—on Christmas Eve I like riding my bike to The Forks with my parents, because the best way to enjoy Christmas is to spend time with your family.

I like the Christmas concerts at school because

the songs we learn are all built into a play. I like hayrides, where we ride on a sleigh pulled by two horses whose coats steam in the cold air, and I get to push other children off the sleigh and to wrestle with them.

I specially like Christmas dinner, with family and friends around me.

Now I'm travelling 3900 kilometres east from Winnipeg to Quebec City, which is where 9-year-old Gage lives (I am retaining his own language, because Canada is a dual-language country). He wrote:

Au Québec, Noël, c'est quand ça neige. Je joue dans la neige avec mon chien, Zoë. On voit del lumières de toutes les couleurs dehors, sur les maisons et dans tous les magasins.

À la maison, on met le sapin, et on décore le sapin.

On voit toute notre famille qui vient de loin, et les amis. On mange un grand diner avec de la dinde et toute notre famille, et on met des bougies sur la table et partout. J'aime bien Noël aussi.

Another 1400 kilometres west of Winnipeg is the province of Alberta, where I received notes from two children. Krista lives in the small town of Dapp, which is a two-hour drive north of the the city of Edmonton. Krista chose to email me a brief comment about her five-year-old sister:

On Christmas Eve, she leaves a plate of chips and dip, and a soda pop for Santa, because my mom has told her that Santa gets sick eating cookies and drinking milk all the time.

And still in Alberta, 120 kilometres southwest of Dapp, 13-year-old Ashley lives in the town of Stony Plain. She wrote:

> *Do you know what I like about Christmas in Stony Plain? During the Christmas week there are sleigh rides, skating at Rotary Park, and free hot chocolate at the Dog Rump Creek Visitors Booth. You see the people dressed all snug, sitting on straw bales placed around an enormous log fire, wrapping their blankets around them and sipping their cocoa, waiting for the sleigh rides to return.*
>
> *What they don't know is a huge surprise awaits them, for as the sleigh approaches there is a shout of "3...2...1, FIRE!" Snowballs, piled up by the children on the sleigh, fly everywhere!*

Back across the ocean now, to Lloyd, who lives in Vanderbajlpark, South Africa:

> *I like putting up all the decorations and looking at the nice colourful lights. The thing that I wish we could have is snow. But the nice thing in South Africa is that we can swim and go on holiday in Durban. It's nice to open presents, but I feel sorry for the orphans and street kids because they don't get any.*

Many people living in hot countries tell me they wish for snow, but have no idea what it's like to shovel all that heavy white stuff for five months of the year! Mariah's view, as a person who sees more snow than most of us, is much more accepting. She lives in Aspen, Colorado, which is a favourite ski resort and so is well-known as snow country:

In the winter the trees are covered with snow - it's really pretty and Christmassy.

My family opens presents in the morning of Christmas Day: it's very much a family thing. Have you given somebody a present and you get to enjoy watching them, being Santa for them, and being happy for a really long time?

Laura and Neil were lodging in the same Bed and Breakfast that I was staying in while on holiday in England, and I met them and their parents in the lounge on several evenings after dinner. Laura is 11 and Neil is 8, and Laura told me they live in Hillingdon, Middlesex, which is quite close to London.

When I mentioned that I was thinking about writing a story containing children's views of Christmas from around the world, Laura started right away telling me what Christmas is like where she and Neil live. So in this piece, she didn't *write* to me, she *told* me (and I made notes):

It always seems to take such a long time for Christmas to come.

There are two things I specially like doing: going carol singing with my friends, walking from house to house in the dark and gazing at the lights their owners display, and attending a school Christmas disco.

Christmas is special because my grandma and grandpa come to have lunch with us on Christmas Day.

Back again to New Zealand, this time to Auckland in the North Island, where I was entertained joyfully by Phillip and Willa and their three children: Hannah, Michael and

Isabella. Michael, full of energy, inveigled me into playing a game of lions with them, crouching behind furniture and leaping out with great roars – yes, me too!

Before leaving to return to Canada, I mentioned that I was planning to write a story about children at Christmas, and invited one of them to contribute. Several weeks later I received this letter:

Hello! It's me, Hannah (the oldest lion, now 10). I'm doing okay at school and at home. Here is my Christmas sort-of on tape, but for you to read: Well, first my brother, sister and me, well we play, play and play.

What is special about our Christmas is that our family is together and mum and dad are home most of the time. Probably the best thing about Christmas is that I do not have to go to school and also I don't have to do homework. My mum and dad usually make phone calls to my uncles and aunts and friends all around the world. I like to listen to my parents talking to the other person on the line from another phone in the house (yes, it is allowed).

It is fairly hot at Christmas time and it is dry as well as being hot (25 degrees C). Our lunch and dinner are big. We have ham, chicken (sometimes roast turkey), salad, rice, fish, prawns, and other yummy dishes.

During the week before Christmas we go to rest homes in little groups and sing carol songs for the old people who live there. We usually sing about six or seven songs and go to two homes in the same day.

We have a Christmas tree, which we store in the garage, amongst all the cobwebs, spiders and other little gadgets. I have to fetch it with my dad (I have to do it because my brother and sister are too young), but I hate it because of all the cobwebs and spiders! It's all right when it's in the house and my dad has dusted it off, and then we all help to decorate it. We do not light up our house at all, but we do light up our Christmas tree.

For the last letter I am heading diametrically through the centre of the earth to Bromma in Sweden. Fourteen-year-old Gustaf proved to be a particularly eloquent writer for his age:

In Sweden we celebrate Christmas on December 24th, Christmas Eve. In our family—my mother, sister and myself—we usually spend the holiday season at home. Some days before Christmas we buy a tree (a real fir tree) in the marketplace and carry it home together. We keep it on the balcony so the needles won't come off too soon after we put it up.

On the evening of December 23rd we take the tree in, cooperate in trying to make it stand stable and straight, and my mommy puts electric candles in it and a star at the top. Then my sister and I decorate it with decorations that have been in our family for generations, like granny's glass birds and great-granny's glass spheres. When we are ready, we kids are shooed off to sleep and mummy puts the Christmas gifts under the tree.

When we wake it's Christmas Even. We wake early and rush in to the tree to find the presents (and examine them and try to guess what's inside), but we don't open them until the evening. On the mantelpiece there are two stockings with some small gifts in them for sister and me, an American tradition introduced when we were very small to make us endure the waiting for Santa better.

At noon, father comes (our parents are divorced) and we have our Christmas meal together. In Sweden we have ham, spare ribs, liver paste, meat balls, potatoes, cabbage, herring salad with beetroots, dark bread with raisins, and a lot of other traditional courses.

After that, father gives us his presents (when we were small he used to dress up as Santa, come in "ho-ho-ing", and ask "Are there any nice children here?", which is the standard phrase for every Santa with self esteem). Then daddy leaves to spend the evening with his wife.

We watch Donald Duck and other programs on TV; when we were younger mum read traditional Christmas stories aloud to us, like Tomten, an old figure in Swedish folklore (a sort of small gnome living in a farmhouse who had, oddly enough, developed into a kind of Santa Claus figure during the last century).

In the evening, we have fruit, dates, raisins, nuts and chocolates and soda drinks, although my mummy sips glögg, a kind of Swedish Glühwein, a red wine with almonds and spices.

It's then that my sister, mummy and I open our Christmas gifts together, with a birchwood fire sparkling in the fireplace.

We go to bed quite late and do not very often make it for Early Service in the nearby church the next morning.

~~~

I started these excerpts with a piece from Adele in Guernsey. Now I am returning there, but to seventy years earlier, when I was a child and lived on the island. This little piece came from my very first Christmas letter (and also appeared in my book *Au Revoir, Sarnia Chérie,* in 2000):

Traditionally, the 25th of December is a special day for children in Great Britain, and Guernsey was no exception. Yet it's Christmas Eve that I remember more clearly, because our parents established a simple, warm, family tradition which we repeated year after year.

At about 2:30 p.m. my mother would call to me and my two brothers Tony and Ian: "Come on in from the garden," she would say. We would run in much more readily than we normally might, knowing what was about to happen. "Wash your hands and faces, then get ready to go to town."

She would check that Tony and I were wearing our school blazers above knee-length grey pants, and that Ian had donned his grey-green jersey with his elementary school badge sewn on at chest level. When she was satisfied we looked smart and clean, she would shepherd us down the gravel path into
~~~

La Bellieuse lane and around the corner to the top of Les Merriennes. There we, agog with expectation, would board a bus headed toward St. Peter Port, the island's town centre.

Twenty minutes later the bus would deposit us beside the Town Church, opposite the Victoria Pier, from where we would walk a short distance up the cobblestoned High Street and turn left into the Commercial Arcade—a pedestrian mall lined mainly with clothing, jewellery and shoe shops. Our target, however, was Le Cheminant's, the largest shop in the Arcade, and *a toy shop.*

The shop was situated on a corner and had three wide windows on one side and two on the other. Ian, still holding his mother's hand, would drag her to the middle window on the long side so he could gaze at the model cars and aeroplanes. Tony would detach himself from the group and walk around the corner to gaze wistfully at the boxed sets of oil paints and pastels.

But, as the eldest, I was given little opportunity to window-gaze.

"Walk up to the Press," my mother would say. "Tell your father we're waiting."

I would nod (the procedure was the same every year) and walk sedately—self importantly—through the shoppers until I rounded the corner into the High Street and was out of my mother's view. Then I would break into a trot, stepping nimbly around islanders chatting in small groups or working their way down to the bus stops, until I reached Boots the Chemists. There I would skirt around the edge of Le Riche's grocery shop and push up the steeper slope of Smith Street. Half way up the hill, I would turn into an unmarked door and take the wooden steps up to the editorial office two at a time, pausing at the top for long enough so that, to my father, I wouldn't look as if I had been hurrying—that I wasn't overly excited—when I pushed open the door. (My father was the editor of the local newspaper.)

"Ah!" he would say. "I think I know why you're here."

He would pull on his suit jacket, dig in the pocket for his pipe, and turn to wish a Happy Christmas to any of the editorial staff who were still present (all done agonizingly slowly, I felt) and then we would start the walk back to the Arcade. Everyone in the street seemed to be in a jovial mood and many who knew my father would pause to exchange seasonal greetings. Meanwhile, I would hang around the periphery, mentally urging them to hurry: *this is Christmas Eve*!

Eventually we would turn into the Arcade and immediately I could see Tony standing at the same shop window, still eyeing the painting sets. Ian would release his mother's hand, run up to his father, and drag him to the window to point to the Meccano set he hoped to find at the foot of his bed the next morning. My father would bend down beside him to see exactly what he was pointing at, and then look up briefly, over Ian's head, to exchange a glance with my mother. I would watch carefully, because the slightest nod or shake of the head would tell me whether she had bought what Ian wanted.

"Well, we'll have to see what Father Christmas has in mind," my father would say, then he would release his hand and walk around the corner to Tony, who would point to the box of oil paints he had been admiring .

"Hmmm, we'll have to see," my father would murmur. "Watercolours are easier to work with, don't you think? They dry out so easily and they're lots easier to clean up."

My mother would drag Ian toward us and say: "We should get into Le Noury's, Stan, before it fills up."

Le Noury's was the family's favourite restaurant, famous among adults for its 'steak-and-kidney pie with chips' lunch, but more famous among us boys for its teas.

We'd tramp up the steep stairs, my two young brothers scampering ahead to search for a round table in front of a window so they could look down on the shoppers in the Arcade and, by craning their necks, still see into Le Cheminant's windows 20 feet down the road.

Tea would be a Christmas treat: paste and cress sandwiches cut into little triangles, hot crumpets swimming in rich Guernsey butter, scones with honey or jam, hot mince tarts and thick slices of dark, rich fruit cake topped by a layer of sweet marzipan and crusty royal icing. And then, the moment we boys had been waiting for: the waitress would arrive bearing a two-tiered plate with little white and pink iced cakes with coloured decorations, each sitting daintily inside a white doily (always, a second plate of these delicacies had to be ordered!).

"Just one each," our mother would caution us, but of course she would give in because it was Christmas Eve and my father would call the waitress over to replenish the upper level.

Toward the end of our tea, my father would rest his teacup on its saucer, lay his hands flat on the table, lean toward us, and announce, with a twinkle in his eye (and always with exactly the same words): "Well, boys! You know, I think this is going to be a very special Christmas. The best ever!" And my mother would smile and nod in agreement.

"And tomorrow," he would continue, with his head angled toward our mother, "just remember who spends all day roasting the chicken and preparing the roast potatoes you so like and the Brussels sprouts some of you don't seem to like, and steaming the Chistmas Pudding and making the rich custard that follow."

We would smile and nod in agreement, in mother's direction.

After tea, we would walk past the Town Church and out onto the Victoria Pier, which I now recognize was part of our parents' plan to work off the big meal and partly to calm us down so we would sleep more readily when eased into our beds. Tony would walk in front with me and we would chat amiably as we approached the dozen or so steps leading up to the parapet on the upper level. My parents would stroll behind us, more slowly, reflecting on the comfortableness of their world and their family. My mother would slide her hand through the crook of my father's arm, and little Ian would grasp his other hand.

It would be fully dark by now and we would lean against the low granite wall high above the water and watch the reflected lights from Castle Cornet and the lighthouse at the end of the pier bob up and down in the gently moving sea. The dark shapes of the moored fishing boats would rise and fall slowly among the lights, and their masts would swing gently back and forth all in a concerted movement.

For us children – and for our parents – all was well with the world, for it was a delightful way to usher in Christmas and so start the season of good cheer and goodwill.

The Christmas Eve of 1939 is particularly etched on my memory; I was 14 and my brothers were 12 and 7. Although we had no way of knowing it then, this was the last time we would celebrate the start of Christmas in that special way. We would no longer climb up the steps into the bus, I would no longer race up High Street to fetch my father, Tony and Ian would no longer peer into Le Cheminant's windows, and we would no longer eat our fill at Le Noury's, ushering in Christmas in the way we so relished.

For, six months later, the German armies had marched solidly through western Europe, down the coast of France, and by 30th June 1940 had taken over the Channel Islands—the only British territory to be occupied during World War II. By then we had been evacuated—first we three boys

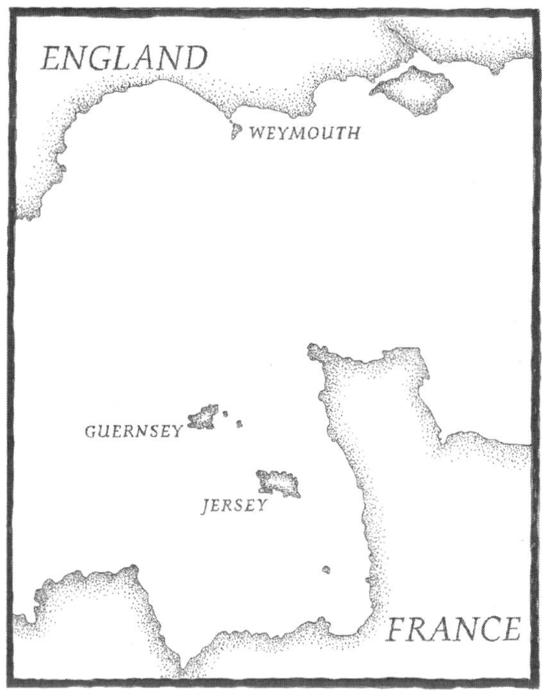

with our school, Elizabeth College (together with countless other schools), and then a few days later by our parents—to Lancashire in the northwest of England. The islands were occupied for the following five years, during which the family moved permanently to Winnipeg in Canada, from where I now write my Christmas letters.

My parents never returned to their island, although their three sons have taken their wives and their children to gain hands-on knowledge of their family's heritage. I have been more fortunate, for in recent years I have been able to visit Guernsey at least twice annually, constantly pulled back by the natural beauty of the island, by the call of the sea beating on its shores, and by memories of the island as it was when our family lived there – memories that haunt me to this day.

4

A Christmas Visitor

Whenever I hear the classic Christmas rhyme

'Twas the night before Christmas and all through the house,
Not a creature was stirring, not even a mouse...

it reminds me of an incident that unexpectedly ruffled the surface of Raymond Brouard's Christmas preparations.

The Christmas of 2003 proved to be unique for Raymond, when a visitor unknown to him swooped down from way up north—almost from the north pole—and dropped in for a brief stopover. (No, I'm afraid it wasn't Santa Claus!) When he told me how it happened, I thought the circumstances were intriguing and they certainly had a unique outcome.

Raymond is a widower who lives alone in a bungalow close to a shopping mall known as Grant Park, in Winnipeg. He has three adult children and, he tells me, four grandchildren ("Although I'm never quite sure, because the numbers keep changing – I mean they keep increasing."), many of whom would be joining him for a celebratory family dinner on Christmas Day.

Raymond has a well-founded reputation as an accomplished cook, among both family and friends. More, he loves to host dinners and revels in setting an elegant table, which he sets at least two days in advance so he can admire it and tweak the positions of napkins, cutlery and decorations as he prepares and cooks the meal.

His attention to detail—his need to ensure that everything is 'just right'—is not surprising: before he retired three years ago, Raymond was chief auditor for a major financial institution.

"You know what that's like," our mutual friend Ben Stollard reminds me. "He has to know where every penny goes: that everything in those long, long columns of figures is accounted for."

Raymond just smiles and shrugs: "That's the way it has to be," he says in his quiet way.

He pays similar attention to his dress, even when he drops into the local mall to buy a loaf of bread: always, he is tidily dressed in grey slacks with a sharp crease down the front, as though he has just ironed them, topped by a cream shirt and V-neck pullover of a contrasting colour, often a light beige.

~~~

I first heard about Raymond's fly-in visitor from a CBC radio news clip on Boxing Day. I didn't phone him immediately, because I suspected he would be besieged by telephone calls from others who had heard it. I knew I would be seeing him personally the following day, when he and I would be joining four friends for a post-Christmas lunch at Ben's apartment, now an annual tradition.

"My visitor's name was Kathryn," Raymond explained in answer to our questions, "and she was no one I
~~~

knew personally."

He said he had heard her name for the first time just four days ago, shortly after 10 a.m. on Tuesday, December 23rd. He was pushing a shopping cart through the Grant Park Safeway, into which he had already deposited a leg of ham, a poly bag of Brussels sprouts, white potatoes for roasting, and a pre-cooked Christmas pudding. He was about to select a package of Christmas crackers ("the kind you pull," he explained, "not the kind you eat"), when he felt the vibrator in his cell phone. He paused and lifted the phone to his ear.

"Raymond Brouard speaking."

"Hello, Raymond; this is Matthew, calling from England."

"Oh … Hi, Matthew. What a surprise! Merry Christmas." Matthew is Raymond's nephew, on his deceased wife's side of the family.

"And the same to you, Raymond."

Raymond was momentarily concerned: a Christmas call from Matthew's mother (she is Raymond's sister-in-law) would have been normal, almost expected, at this time of year. But a call from her eldest son seemed to portend bad news.

"Is everything all right?" Raymond asked, trying to keep the concern from showing in his voice.

"Oh, yes. I talked to mother today and she is well, as we all are."

Raymond paused in his story to explain that he has several nephews and nieces on his wife's side of the family, and most of them live in pretty villages and towns along the Thames Valley, west of London. (I would have liked to ask his wife Emily how much she missed the gently winding river backed by rolling hills; Manitoba's flat expanses must have seemed endless and dull in comparison. Yet I never knew her well enough to venture posing the question.)

"I wonder," Matthew continued, "if you would mind doing me a favour."

"Of course."

Matthew told him that a family friend—Kathryn—had been flying from Vancouver to London Heathrow overnight, when she became ill over Hudson Bay. Two doctors who happened to be on the Boeing 747 attended her and suspected she might be having a stroke or a heart attack. They told a flight attendant that she urgently needed medical attention, more than they could provide within the confined space and limited facilities of a jumbo jet. She relayed the information to the captain, who decided to turn south and land at the nearest major airport, which happened to be Winnipeg. Within minutes of touching down—it was then 3 a.m.—Kathryn had been whisked off to the nearby Grace Hospital.

"Is that hospital anywhere near where you live?" Matthew asked.

"Absolutely," Raymond said. "About 5 kilometres—no more than 3 miles."

"Is there any chance you could drive over there and find out how Kathryn is? Then phone me back so I can inform her parents? They are my neighbours and they're sick with worry."

Raymond agreed that he would (actually, what he said in his somewhat laconic way, was "No problem."). Then he looked down at his nearly-full shopping cart and realized he must first check out. The groceries would be able to stay in his car, because with Winnipeg winter temperatures the trunk was like a highly efficient refrigerator, or more often a freezer.

When he walked through the sliding doors of the Grace Hospital and introduced himself to the receptionist, she knew immediately why he was there, indicated that he was expected, and asked an orderly to take him down to the scanning unit. There, he saw a youngish woman lying on a platform about to be slid into an ultrasound scanner. The technician paused and stood back, gesturing for Raymond to approach.

Raymond introduced himself and asked if she was indeed Kathryn.

"Yes," she said somewhat hesitantly. "I am."

Raymond explained that he was visiting her on behalf of Matthew and her parents.

"Oh, that's wonderful," she said. "But how on earth did you know I was here?"

He described his relationship to Matthew and the telephone conversation they had had just an hour ago.

"He's such a dear," Kathryn said, and then added quickly. "If I give you my parents' number, could you phone and tell them I'm all right? That I'm not at death's door?"

He agreed that he would.

"Oh, thank you. They worry so much; they always do."

Raymond told us that Kathryn looked pale, a little drawn, but was lucid and clear-headed. He estimated she was about 30, possibly 35: "It was difficult to tell."

She told him she had been given medication and already was feeling brighter. The pain was gone, but the hospital needed to carry out further checks to determine what had caused her sudden distress on board the airliner.

The technician was ready to slide Kathryn into the scanner, so ushered Raymond out of the room and down the hall to meet Kathryn's doctor. She explained that the incident seemed to have been prompted by the patient being overwrought from work, plus some personal problems before she boarded the flight, which caused her to hyperventilate and have difficulty breathing. The symptoms had eased once she was at ground level, and particularly since being admitted to the emergency room.

The doctor added that by late afternoon she would have a full analysis of the tests Kathryn had been put through and would then decide whether she was to be admitted or released. She recommended that Raymond come back at 4 p.m.

On the way out to his car, Raymond called Matthew and relayed the details he had learned, concurrently assuring him that Kathryn was in good hands and seemed to be in better shape than he had expected.

Matthew sounded relieved: "I'll pop in next door and tell her parents, save you from having to call them."

So Raymond returned to Grant Park, completed his shopping, drove home, and stored his purchases. Then, feeling "a bit discombobulated," he decided to start setting his dining table for the family dinner he would be hosting on Christmas Day.

"But I kept wondering," he told us, "how I would feel if this had happened to my Melissa."

Raymond's daughter has been teaching in Kuwait for the past three years. She flies home twice a year, and always for New Year's.

"I mean: suppose, when she is flying here the day after tomorrow, I get a telephone call to say Melissa is ill and the plane has flown her into Marseilles instead of carrying her through to Toronto. It would be bad enough knowing she was so sick that the plane had to make an emergency landing. But thinking of her in a strange city in a strange country, and how alone she would feel.... Ugh!... And at this distance I would be so unable to help."

We all nodded in agreement, thinking of our own

children—particularly our daughters—if this were to happen to them.

When he returned to the hospital, the receptionist ushered him into a private reception room where he found Kathryn sitting in a wheelchair with her coat on and her suitcase resting on the floor beside her.

"They're letting me out," she said.

"You *need* to be in a wheelchair?"

"Standard procedure, I guess." She grinned. "I have to be signed for, like I'm being let out of prison!"

Raymond laughed. "Back to the airport, then?"

"No, no. The hospital has made arrangements…"

At that moment the same doctor Raymond had spoken to earlier appeared with paperwork for Kathryn to sign.

"Discharge papers?" Kathryn asked, as she lowered the doctor's pen onto the paper.

The doctor nodded and, unaware of the underlying humour, turned to Raymond: "Kathryn is clear to leave. We've booked her into a motel on Portage Avenue, on Air Canada's instructions. She is to wait there until a decision is made as to whether she is to continue her flight to England."

"In a *motel*?" Raymond was appalled. "You mean, she is to sit alone in a motel, after all that has happened!"

"Those were our instructions…," the doctor started.

"No way!" Raymond turned to Kathryn: "You're coming home with me. Christmas is *not* the time to be on your own in a seedy airport motel!"

"Oh, that will be so much better," the doctor said, clearly relieved that she wasn't discharging her patient into personal solitude. "If you will give me your address and phone number I will inform Air Canada."

Raymond threw Kathryn's suitcase onto the back seat of his car, held the front passenger door open for her to climb in, and drove her to his home, the car bumping over the rutted, ice-covered streets.

In the house, Kathryn showed him the documentation she had been given, which contained the requirement that she must wait in Winnipeg until the Air Canada medical staff in Montreal had decided whether she was to fly onward. First they had to examine the records being forwarded from Grace Hospital, and then confer with the airline's legal department.

"What if they won't let me fly?" She was almost in tears. "I don't want to go back to Vancouver. And if I have to, it will mean going by a Greyhound bus, and I'm not at all keen on that."

"A train, more likely: you would be much more comfortable."

Raymond handed her a box of Kleenex. "Anyway, just take one step at a time," he added, always the pragmatist. "If you're not allowed to fly right away, then you can stay here and have Christmas with the family. We'd really like that."

He was perfectly sincere in saying so; he knew, just as I do, that his family would immediately welcome her and make her feel part of their scene.

"Look," he continued, "why don't you try to get some sleep? And don't even *think* about the alternatives until this evening, until after you have heard from Air Canada."

Kathryn was weary and tried to sleep, but only intermittently because she was apprehensive about the decision.

The call came shortly after seven. Raymond handed her the mobile phone.

Her demeanour as she listened—a quick nod and smile in his direction—told him right away that it was good news. Then she covered the mouthpiece for a moment and asked for a pencil and paper.

"The Air Canada medics feel it's safe for me to continue

on to London!" she announced as she handed the mobile back to him. "I have to be at the Air Canada counter at noon tomorrow."

She showed him the details: her flight would leave Winnipeg at 1:30 with a connection in Toronto to flight 856 for Heathrow.

"Which means you will arrive in London really early on Christmas Day." Raymond had already calculated the times. "So you *will* be home in time for Christmas!"

The next day—Christmas Eve—shortly before noon Raymond strode up to the Air Canada counter carrying her suitcase, with Kathryn trying to keep up with him.

"Ah, yes," the gate attendant said, turning to address her directly. "We know all about you."

At first Kathryn thought he was being critical of her, but was relieved when he explained that everything had been prepared for her to travel, and he just needed to see her passport. He tagged her luggage, inserted a red pointer flag so that it stuck out from the tag, pushed a button so the suitcase moved onto the rolling luggage carrier, and handed Kathryn her tickets.

"Here's a pass to the executive lounge," he added, "so you can wait in comfort. And I wish you a successful and comfortable flight."

Then he handed another pass to Raymond. "This will let you in through security, and into the executive lounge, so you can accompany your guest right to the gate."

"I guess Air Canada wants to make sure I *do* get on the plane," Kathryn quipped as they rode the escalator up to the departures level. "And look at this, they've booked me into first class, *all the way*! Seats 2A and 5G."

Raymond turned to us: "So, you see, it all worked out."

I smiled privately, remembering two more lines

from the last stanza of the Christmas poem *The Night Before Christmas:*

> He sprang to his sleigh, to his team gave a whistle,
> And away they all flew, like the down of a thistle.

But Raymond's lunchtime audience would not let him stop there: they insisted he must explain the story they had heard on the morning news.

"Well, yes," Raymond laughed. "I remember thinking, as I wandered out to my car, that Kathryn's departure was the end of the story. But, as you know, it wasn't."

Raymond said he was up early the following morning—Christmas Day—to prepare dinner for his family, who would start arriving mid-afternoon. Then, just as he was pushing spoonfuls of celery-and-mushroom stuffing into the cavernous interior of a 21-pound turkey, his front doorbell rang.

"Oh, no," he said. "Someone's here already!"

Raymond had already received five telephone calls from England that morning: from Kathryn and her parents, from Matthew, from Matthew's mother, and from two more of his in-laws. And these were on top of several greetings from his family. It was becoming increasingly difficult to keep abreast of his dinner-preparation schedule!

He wiped his hands cursorily on a paper towel and peeked through the eye-hole in the front door: he did not recognize the casually dressed man and woman standing on the top step. With hands still sticky from the turkey, he used the paper towel to turn the door-handle.

"You are Raymond Brouard?" the woman asked.

Raymond acknowledged that he was.

"Merry Christmas," she said. "We're from the *Winnipeg Free Press* and we want to get some more information about a visitor who was diverted from an Air Canada flight two days ago. Could you spare a moment to help us?"

Raymond explained that he was preparing the dinner and really was far too busy.

"Oh, it won't take more than a couple of minutes. And we can talk to you while you continue doing… whatever you need to do."

Raymond shrugged and stepped back so they could enter: it was far too cold to keep talking with the front door open. As they followed him into the kitchen, she introduced the man who had accompanied her as a *Free Press* photographer.

"I should have known right away that I was making a mistake," Raymond told us. "But by then it was too late."

The reporter's questions were mostly to confirm the name of the person who was delayed, learn how she came to stay with Raymond, and obtain her phone number in England.

"What was the connection between you and this 'Kathryn'?" she asked.

"None, really." Raymond briefly described the phone call from his nephew and how he lived next-door to Kathryn's parents.

"Well, thank you," the journalist snapped her notebook shut. "That's just what I need." Then she added: "Oh, it would be nice if we could have a photograph of you, now that we're here."

Raymond said no: "I'm not appropriately dressed and anyway my hands are sticky from handling the turkey."

He explained to us that he hadn't shaved and was wearing an apron already splattered with grease over an ancient track suit with holes in the knees.

Then the photographer stepped forward: "That's a good-looking bird," he said, pointing to the turkey on the counter, "weighs about 20 pounds I should think."

Raymond acknowledged he was correct, within a pound.

"Well, why don't you try holding the turkey up for the

picture: like a symbol of the season?"

Raymond agreed, just to get the journalist and photographer out of the house as quickly as possible. He held the turkey in front of him on its metal tray, and with two quick flashes the photographer had done his work. Then they were gone and Raymond returned to his preparations, even later than planned but still secure that with the family's help the dinner and day would be a success.

The next morning, Raymond said, he was wakened at 7:30 by the first of several telephone calls that came crowding in from Winnipeg friends, with each urging him to read the front page of the Boxing Day newspaper.

"But no one would tell me why! If I didn't have a paper, they kept saying, then get out there and buy one!"

So after lunch Raymond trudged through the snow to the local convenience store, where the couple who run the shop greeted him with broad smiles: "Well, Merry Christmas, Mr. Brouard: you *are* in distinguished company!"

Raymond was puzzled.

Seeing his discomfort, the woman stepped out from behind the counter and over to the magazine rack against the wall. She pulled out a copy of that morning's *Winnipeg Free Press*, unfolded it, and held it up so Raymond and everyone else in the shop could see.

Three photographs filled the front page: on the left, one of Pope John Paul II arriving at St. Peter's Basilica in the Vatican; on the right, one of Queen Elizabeth II walking into the Church of St. Mary Magdalene at Sandringham, in England; and in the middle, sandwiched between the other two photographs, one of a grinning Raymond holding his turkey.

The shop owner read aloud the caption below it: "The Winnipegger who hosted an unexpected guest on Christmas

Eve displays his holiday turkey."

Everyone in the store clapped, much to Raymond's embarrassment.

"When I saw the silly grin on my face," he said, "I wished I hadn't let that photographer poke his camera at me." (Although he did admit the turkey looked inviting.)

When he went to pay for the paper, the woman wouldn't let him: "You're the only person in the city who is ever likely to share the front page with the Pope and the Queen!" she said. "How could I?"

Ben reached into his magazine rack, pulled out a copy of the paper, and read to us:

CHRISTMAS IN PICTURES

Woman amazed by city's yule spirit

It was two days before Christmas and a stranger needed a bed for the night.

The woman in distress wasn't riding a donkey, but a plane, diverted to Winnipeg after she fell ill...

"It completely restored my faith in humanity that so many people were so kind to a complete stranger," she said in a phone interview from her parents' home in England on Christmas Day.

Describing her night stop in Winnipeg, she continued: "You don't expect that kind of kindness from a complete stranger; it's one of those things you see in a Christmas story."

We all applauded, again much to Raymond's embarrassment.

DOUGHN

5

To Florida for Christmas

I heard of the Christmas experience described in this chapter following a Heritage Group meeting at Red River College in Winnipeg. The Heritage Group is composed entirely of College retirees, of whom I am one (I taught technical communication skills to engineering technology students, and observation writing to Child Care Services students, for the 23 years leading up to my retirement)

We meet once a month, first for a brief business meeting and then to listen to a guest speaker who offers advice on topics ranging from making one's own wine, through finding the most advantageous travel insurance, to describing a unique travel experience.

Following a recent meeting, the co-chairs invited me to join them for lunch in the Prairie Lights Dining Room, which is part of the Culinary Arts and Hotel/Motel Management course at the College, and is staffed by students who are learning to cook excellent restaurant meals and serve them elegantly.

Our student server was a moderately tall, slim, dark-haired young woman, about 18-20, who carried herself well with a purposeful demeanour, yet with a ready smile. Somehow she seemed familiar, as though I had met her before, but I couldn't place her.

At the end of the meal, however, she came up to me as I was leaving the table: "Are you…?" she asked, stating my name.

I agreed that I was.

"My Dad was talking about you, just last week."

She noticed some hesitation on my part: "Myles Reddish," she explained.

"Myles! Of course. Then you must be Debbie."

She smiled in agreement.

"I thought I recognized you… but I wasn't sure… "

She laughed and handed me a slip of paper with a phone number on it. "Give Dad a call, will you. He'd like to see you, to keep in touch."

Myles and I met at Starbucks on Corydon Avenue the following week. We see each other only rarely, but when we do we cover a lot of ground!

I have written about Myles and his two daughters before, in Chapter 1. He has been a single parent for close to 12 years now, and from watching Debbie I sensed just what a good parent he has been for her and his younger daughter, Chris.

As I also have been a single parent, we inevitably have interesting anecdotes to exchange. This time Myles described what he and his girls had done the previous Christmas—2009—and again he is telling his own story, as he did earlier in the book.

Myles's Christmas Story

The unusual way in which we (Debbie, Chris and

I) spent last Christmas really started when I came home from work one afternoon last September and found a Manitoba Hydro card in the mailbox. It asked me to read the gas meter and phone in the numbers, so I grabbed a flashlight and descended to the far end of the basement.

To my surprise, all four hands pointed to zero: 0–0–0–0.

This is unbelievable, I thought, and tapped the meter dial, wondering if the meter had stopped working. But, apart from a slight quivering of the four pointers, nothing changed.

So I waited until Debbie came home and asked her to re-check the reading with me. By now the farthest pointer on the right had moved slightly and the meter was reading 0–0–0–1.

I heard the back door bang – typical of Chris's entrances – and heard her call: "Anyone home?"

"We're down here," Debbie shouted up to her. "You've got to see this!"

A moment later Chris came bouncing down the narrow steps, taking them two at a time. She peered up at the dials.

"Dad!" she said in a sort-of stage whisper. "You've got to go right out and buy a lottery ticket."

"It's only a coincidence," I remonstrated. I never buy lottery tickets.

"Today you must: just look at the date!"

"Yeah, Dad. It's the 13th," Debbie chimed in. "You've just got to!"

"And do it right now!" Chris was pulling on my arm. "Before your luck runs out."

So up to the mall we went and I gave the cashier sufficient money to buy seven tickets: three for each girl and one for me.

"No, Dad," Debbie insisted. "Three for you, too."

She dug into her purse and plonked some more coins onto the counter. "Three!" she announced to the attendant, "and one of them is going to be a winner!"

And on Saturday night she was proved right, to the tune of $4700, and on one of my tickets!

The girls insisted I spend the money strictly on myself:

"You're always buying stuff for us, Dad," Debbie said. "It's time for you to use the money for something you would like."

And Chris nodded vigorously.

"Alright! Alright!" I admit I was being a bit defensive. "I'll think about it. Just give me time."

Yet I really did want to share the winning with the girls: we had lived like that, sharing equally, for over ten years.

I knew Debbie could use the money for books she would have to buy next month, for the second year of her course at Red River College. As for Chris: she is so fashion-conscious—has to be right up to the mark with her peers—I knew she would love to go on a shopping spree.

So I sat on the idea.

But only for five days, when a letter from the Canadian Automobile Association prompted me to move. The CAA was offering an all-inclusive Christmas special, ten days in Florida, including tickets to Disneyworld, at a very attractive price.

Maybe we should do something different this year, I thought, take in the sights, lie around the pool, enjoy the warm sun, and pull oranges right off the tree!

But it wouldn't be all that easy, because it would mean breaking with tradition. We wouldn't be visiting my sister in Minnedosa on Christmas Eve, as we had done since the girls were little; we wouldn't wake up to a white scene outside our windows on Christmas morning; and we wouldn't be able to gather around the tree which, every year, we drove together into the country to cut ourselves, and the girls always so painstakingly and joyously decorated.

Much as the idea might appeal to her, I knew Chris would resist. At 16, as she was then, she had become a compulsive, challenging young teen; yet hidden underneath the bravado I knew a traditional young girl still lurked.

I knew exactly what Debbie would say: "Yes, let's." But could I be sure she wasn't saying it just to make me happy? Debbie is good at reining in her true feelings.

I pondered whether I should discuss the idea with them before making the booking, then decided to do it on my own and "ride out" their eventual reaction.

There was more to this than I have implied. I mean, how much longer could I really expect the three of us to continue doing things together, as a family? Debbie needed to start going her own way, not keep holding back and accepting my choices. She, more than Chris, was aware of the pain I had endured twelve years ago, when their mother chose to leave us.

So I made the booking and waited for the confirmation to come from the CAA. Then I printed it and showed it to the girls.

Silence, for several seconds.

"That's a great idea, Dad."

That was Debbie of course. But was her voice superficially enthusiastic? I could not tell.

"Oh, but what about...?" and Chris defiantly reeled off the list of things we usually do over the Christmas season.

"Oh, we'll still do them," I said, "but early: on the weekend before Christmas."

As the weeks elapsed and Christmas grew nearer, I could see that Debbie was genuinely pleased with the idea (although I suspected she may have been 'reading my thoughts' in her quiet way, aware that in time she would want to pull away, assert herself). Even Chris began to display excitement and increased the number of hours she worked at Timmy's, so she could earn extra shopping money to spend in Florida.

~~~
~~~

It all worked perfectly. The flights were direct charters and we were well-treated aboard. The Orlando hotel was close to the Disney village and ran a frequent shuttle over to the Disney complex, and the weather—though not as warm as I had surmised—still prompted the girls to take a chilly swim while the sun was shining onto the pool.

Already I had decided Christmas Day should be a very different experience. Rather than sit around the hotel wondering what was happening in Winnipeg, we would take a full day at Disneyworld, with access to major events and special-day meals in restaurants rather than just "happy meals."

And it worked. We paraded from pavilion to pavilion, snacking along the way but finishing up at supper time in the British pavilion, where they served traditional English Christmas fare. After that we teamed up with two other Winnipeg families to watch the firework display, accompanied by "Ooohs" and "Aaahs" from adults and teens alike.

It was close to midnight when we stood in line, waiting for the shuttle to take us back to the hotel. In a unanimous moment, my daughters—one on each side—linked an arm through one of mine. Debbie leaned closer, her head against my shoulder, murmuring: "So, good.... So, good... I'll remember this day for ever." And even Chris, not the type to outwardly show affection, whispered: "Thanks, Dad. You were so right."

~~~

At breakfast the next morning I announced a
~~~

special plan I had in mind for Boxing Day: "I've rented a car and we're going to drive to a beach north of St Augustine, on the Atlantic coast."

Chris lifted her head sharply from her cereal, her spoon poised in mid-air between the bowl and her mouth. "Why?"

"There's something special I want you to see."

"I can't, Dad. I'm going shopping with Marnie and Tracey."

"You can do that tomorrow," I countered.

"No! You and Deb can go. I'll stay in Orlando."

I'm not good at this, I remember thinking. Oh, Chris, I'm not accustomed to the challenges teens like you can exert! (Debbie had been much more compliant at that age.)

There was a long pause with all three of us sitting very still.

"Chris," I ventured quietly, "I really would prefer..."

"No, no, no!" she shouted and threw her spoon into her cereal dish, pushed her chair back, and flounced out of the room, slamming the bedroom door behind her.

"Oh, dear..."

Deb reached across the table and placed a hand over one of mine. "Give her time, Dad. Let her cool down, then I'll go in and talk to her."

"You shouldn't have to do this."

"You know how she is, always testing. She'll

come round." And she squeezed my hand.

Thirty minutes later Debbie closed the girls' bedroom door behind her. After another twenty minutes they both came back into the main room.

"All right, Dad. I'll phone Marnie and Tracey. Tell them we'll shop on Sunday."

"Thanks, Chris. I appreciate it." I wondered how much Chris's change of heart had cost Debbie, emotionally.

~~~

We set off in a Toyota Corolla at 10 a.m,, heading west at first, toward Daytona Beach. When we reached the coast I turned the car north along a minor road toward St Augustine. "And Kelsey Bay is another 45 minutes past it," I announced.

"Why Kelsey Bay? What's there?"

"There's something special happening; something I'd like you to see."

"You told us that before, Dad."

"I want it to be a surprise."

I knew neither of them was satisfied with that, yet even though they kept probing, I still chose to keep the idea to myself. I think I was afraid Chris would hang her head and mumble something like: "We've come all this way to see that!" And then curl up into a discontented ball on the back seat.

So, where was I taking them? I had read in the local community paper that members of the Kelsey Bay Marine Research and Rescue Program
~~~

would be releasing a seal back into the sea, after rescuing it in a near-death condition five months ago. They had given it medical treatment and fed it until it was well enough to return to its natural environment.

I did an online search at the hotel and learned that the Kelsey Rescue Program was a voluntary group of dedicated individuals who rescued coastal wildlife that had little chance of survival. Often they spent months bringing each seal or turtle back to a healthy condition.

Kelsey Bay is an inlet fed by a small river and is protected from the surging waves of the Atlantic Ocean by a sea wall that almost encloses the inlet.

As I turned in toward the bay I could see a group of about 60 people gathered near the water's edge, standing behind waist-high yellow bands denoting a cordoned-off area. Inside, several men and women of varying ages chatted, each wearing a red sweatshirt announcing their affiliation with the Rescue Program.

Immediately, of course, Debbie and Chris wanted to know what was going on and finally I told them. To my surprise Chris didn't deride the idea; she just reached into her bag and pulled out her video camera.

We walked toward the group and stood on the periphery. At the same moment a light pickup truck backed in, carrying a dark green box with open wire-mesh sides. There was movement within it and a moment later we could see a dark grey seal, about the size of a 10-year-old boy, turning back

and forth with water splashing up from the bottom of the box, put there to keep the seal's coat damp.

"You can see the seal is excited," a young woman who seemed to be moderating the event announced. "He can smell the sea, which he has not been exposed to for five months."

Four members of the group grabbed rope handles, one at each top corner of the box, lifted the box carefully over the lowered tailgate, carried it to the water's edge, and laid it gently on the pebbles.

"We call this seal Busby," the woman continued. "When he was brought to us by a local fisherman, there was real doubt he would survive. He was diseased, had been injured, and weighed only 30 pounds. Today we are proud of him, for he now weighs 85 pounds and is perfectly fit for release back into the sea – his natural environment."

It was at that moment I realized Chris was no

longer standing beside me. For a moment I feared she had walked disconsolately back to the car, and glanced back to see if she had.

But Debbie nudged me with her elbow and pointed ahead and to the right. There was Chris, standing right up against the yellow band! She must have wormed her way forward, no doubt stepping on toes, to the very front of the viewers.

The moderator nodded to one of the volunteers, who leaned forward and opened a gate on the seaward side of the box. Simultaneously, Chris ducked down under the restraining band and ran up to the water's edge, her video camera held to her eye.

"No, no!" The moderator placed a hand on Chris's arm. "It's not safe for you to be in here. That's why we ask you to stay behind..."

"Oh, please. Please," Chris implored her. "I'm from the Canadian Prairies and there will never be another chance like this for me." Chris has a winsome, hard-to-resist smile, which she beamed toward the moderator.

There was a moment's hesitation, and then the woman turned to her: "Alright, then. We'll call you our official photographer from Canada. But stay right beside me and be ready to duck back the moment I tell you."

Already the seal was lurching its way out of the box in an up-and-down movement, dipping its snout into the water. It eased slowly forward until it was half-immersed, and then it paused and looked back at its saviours, as if it was wondering whether it should go farther.

The moderator laughed. "He's not sure whether he wants to lose being fed three times a day. I guess he knows now he will have to find and sometimes fight for everything he wants to eat."

A moment later the seal turned toward the deeper water and pushed ahead until it was fully afloat. We lost sight of it for about 15 seconds, and then saw it surface some 50 yards out from the shore. It lifted its head clear of the rippling waves, looked toward the gathered crowd, shook its head as if acknowledging thanks to its helpers, and then turned out to sea, dipped its nose, and with a flip of its tail vanished from view. The crowd applauded.

The moderator pointed to the video camera in Chris's hand: "Will you email me a copy?"

"Of course." And they exchanged addresses.

On the drive back to Orlando, the girl who had sat grumpily on the back seat on the way out had been exchanged for a never-stop-chattering young woman sitting in the right-hand seat beside me (the girls religiously take turn and turn about, with one sitting up front and one reclining or sleeping on the rear seat.)

Chris didn't need to say "Hey, Dad, that was great!" I knew she thought it was. And my thinking was corroborated by Debbie, who responded with a complicit grin when I glanced up at the rear-view mirror.

~~~

It's ten months since we watched the seal being released back into the sea. Debbie, as you know, is enrolled in the second year of the culinary arts program at Red River College, and doing well. And Chris is still working part-time, but not at Tim
~~~

Hortons. In fact she has two jobs, and is enthusiastic about both of them. Part of the time she volunteers at Fort Whyte Alive Recreational Centre, and the remaining time—the bigger proportion, really—she works at the wildlife interpretative centre at Oak Hammock Marsh, north of Winnipeg. At both she works with wildlife and is enthusiastic about everything she does there.

And there is even more, for she has joined the Canadian Wildlife Federation and inveigled me into becoming a financial contributor!

I guess my choice of a Florida holiday at Christmas was... well...just right.

6

A Delayed Christmas

An unexpected and bittersweet sequence of incidents occurred on Christmas Day of 2010.

I was sitting in the crowded departure lounge at Gate 28 of Terminal 3 in London's Heathrow airport when two teenagers approached, each with a tightly filled backpack slung between their shoulders and carrying some smaller items they had bought in Duty Free. They looked at me a little pointedly, for I was sitting in the middle of three seats with an empty seat on either side, so I folded up my book and moved to my left to make room for them.

"Thank you," they both said as they sat in turn. I suspected immediately from their voices that they must be British children flying to Canada for a visit, not Canadian children returning home. Similarly, their mode of dress was unusual and certainly not Canadian. It was apparent they were wearing school uniforms, evident from the initials WCC embroidered on the breast pocket of the boy's blazer and the girl's cardigan, both a dark olive-green. The boy was wearing black dress pants and the girl a pleated green-and-black skirt over black leotards (like most English girls who wear a school uniform, she had rolled her skirt up at the waist so that the hem ended some 5 cm above her knees, which I imagined was contradictory to her school's knee-length regulation).

Most of my assumptions were corroborated shortly after, when they decided it was alright to talk to the seemingly dull person sitting next to them and explained that WCC stood for Warwickshire County College. (The girl later confided to me that it wasn't *their* idea to travel in school uniform, but their mother's, and that they couldn't really argue because the trip was a Christmas present from their parents.) The girl also volunteered that she was 11 and her brother had just turned 13.

"Although almost everyone says he looks older than that, more like 15 or 16," she continued. "Don't you think I already look like I'm 13, too?"

I agreed that she certainly did, which raised a pleasant smile, just for a moment.

I had already noticed something odd about their demeanour: just when I thought they would be elated to be flying west with Air Canada on a long-distance journey to Calgary, they didn't seem happy; in fact they looked downright despondent—really, really glum. I soon found out why.

"Were you delayed, too?" the girl asked.

I agreed that I had been. For six days.

"Oh, we were only four days." That was the boy.

We had all been held up by the vicious ice storm that struck western Europe on December 19th and effectively shut down not only Heathrow but all the airports in England's southern counties. I was trapped on the Channel Island of Guernsey (which, if you are going to be held up by weather, is a far more comfortable place to be than sitting for hours in crowded Heathrow airport); the boy and girl were stuck in their home in the Midlands, unable to get to London. All the airlines serving Heathrow had to re-book their passengers, and eventually I was told I had been re-scheduled to fly to Canada at 1:15 p.m. on Christmas Day, with a night stop-over in Calgary, Alberta, and a continuing flight to Winnipeg early in the morning of Boxing Day, December 26th. Apparently the same had happened to the two young people sitting beside me.

They introduced themselves as Torrance and Jasmyn, and took care to spell out their names.

"They are a bit unusual," Torrance said. "Our parents originally were from Jamaica—although Jasmyn and I were both born in England—and they chose names that 'have a history' in the family."

"Actually, you can call Torrance 'Tory'," Jasmyn piped up. "Everyone does."

I enquired of Tory whether he was bothered by the inevitable political association with his shortened name.

"I'm used to it. People make a joke about it at first, but when they see I'm not bothered by it they give up."

"Actually, they feel a bit silly for commenting," said Jasmyn, and she erupted into a giggle. Suddenly I could see the happy girl hiding behind her glum exterior, and wondered why she and her brother seemed so down-in-the-mouth.

Jasmyn explained, without my asking: "We were supposed to fly to Toronto last Tuesday, but our flight was cancelled."

"Because of the ice storm?" I asked.

"Yes."

"So this is your Christmas present?" I asked.

"*This?*" Jasmyn stretched out her arms and pointed to the

rows of passengers crowded around us. "No way!"

Tory rested a hand on her arm. "Easy, Jaz." He said it gently, quietly. "I think Jasmyn is referring to the Christmas party we were going to, specially planned for today."

"With our friends in Winnipeg." Jasmyn chimed in. "We were supposed to be there four days ago!"

"Last Tuesday," Tory explained. "The 21st."

"Now we won't be there until Boxing Day."

"Tomorrow?" I asked.

"By then Christmas will be all over!" Jasmyn was on the verge of tears.

"Air Canada says they will fly us from Calgary to Winnipeg tomorrow," Tory continued. "And they'll put us in a hotel tonight, in Calgary."

Jasmyn pulled a Kleenex from a pocket in her skirt and blew on her nose.

"Which hotel?" I asked. Already I recognized the scenario that was emerging, and that it was much like mine. I, too, would have to stay in a hotel, there being no seats available on that evening's flight from Calgary to Winnipeg.

"Dunno." Tory shrugged. "They said they'll arrange it when we get to Calgary. Someone from Air Canada will meet us when we get off the plane."

"I don't *want* to be in a hotel, Tory. *Not on Christmas day*!"

Tory shrugged: "There's nothing we can do about it."

I sensed Jasmyn was again on the edge of tears and wondered if I could persuade Air Canada to lodge them in the Delta hotel, right at the airport, where I had pre-booked a room. There I could at least arrange to have dinner with them in the lounge, rather than leave them sitting in a lonely room in an unfamiliar hotel.

But I had no chance to 'air' my thought, because at that moment a uniformed official walked up. "Right, you two," she announced. "We're going to board you first. Pick up your stuff and come with me."

They each stood up and hauled a backpack onto a shoulder.

Tory turned to me and smiled: "Perhaps we will see you in Calgary."

"No!" Jasmyn turned to me and waved. "See if you can find us on the plane."

"Sure," I shouted after her. "I'll do that. Where are you sitting?"

They glanced back and shook their heads as they wound their way through the passengers already crowding around the gate, even though rows hadn't yet been called.

Jasmyn is going to be tall, I thought; *already she is up to her brother's height* (when first they introduced themselves, I thought perhaps they were a twin). Both carried themselves upright, without slouching, but there the similarity ended. While Tory moved easily, in a very relaxed way, Jasmyn moved definitely and purposefully, like she knew exactly where she was going, almost as if she carried a 'don't get in my way' attitude. Coupled with her dark, deep-set eyes, which had a sparkling intensity about them, I had the impression she would definitely make her mark on the parts of the world she would inhabit.

I knew it wouldn't be all that difficult to find Tory and Jasmyn. But my first try, about two hours after the jetliner had climbed into the air west of London, took longer than I had expected: the shades had been drawn for passengers watching movies on their back-of-seat TV screens, and it was a l-o-n-g way from my seat in row 9 to their seats, which I found in row 43. And when I finally discerned their recumbent forms, I realized they were fast asleep.

Two-and-a-half hours later I tried again. This time they

were wide awake, sitting upright with trays bearing a scone, a glass jar of Coopers strawberry jam, a small carton of raspberry yoghurt, and a coke in front of them. Jasmine was sitting against the aisle, with Tory next to her.

They grinned when they saw me. Jasmyn pointed her knife at half of her scone, which was spread thick with Devonshire clotted cream and a mound of jam on top. "Would you like some?" she asked. "I've got lots."

"That's very nice of you," I said, and squatted in the aisle beside her, so our heads were at the same level, "but they'll be bringing some for me too, when I go back to my seat."

Jasmyn pointed to a glass on her little table: "I'm having a 'Coke', but don't you ever tell mother!"

"She'd have kittens," Tory added, pointing to his glass. "Mine's Jamaican ginger beer."

"Great stuff!" I said, for I like it too.

"Ugh!" Jasmyn grimaced and took another bite from her scone.

It was clear they were much happier than before and were looking forward to actually being in Canada, even if it was in the wrong place. Eventually I asked where they were staying in Winnipeg.

"With our friends."

"Yes, but where?"

Jasmine looked questioningly at her brother, who shrugged. I tried another approach: "I wondered if it might be near where I live, in River Heights. Have you heard that name before?"

They looked blankly at me. It was clear they hadn't.

Tory leaned toward me, in front of Jasmyn: "I remember it's close to Portage." (He pronounced it *Port-arge.*)

For a moment I was puzzled, then the penny dropped. "Ah! I think you mean Portage Avenue *(but this time I pronounced it Portage, as in 'haulage').* "It's the main road in Winnipeg, running east to west."

"You wrote down the address!" Jasmyn's tone was like a challenge, as if she was confronting Tory. "I saw you write it in your diary...when Mummy read it to you from an email on her iPad."

"I know. I know." Tory's response was like a sigh. I thought fleetingly that Jasmyn must have sounded just like their mother, when she had reason to admonish one of them.

"It's in my suitcase."

"Cle-ver!" Jasmyn pointed down toward her toes. "Right down there, in the hold, under our feet!"

I laughed. "That's just the sort of thing I do, Tory!" I was feeling sorry for him, almost cringing under his younger sister's criticism. "Like leaving the key *inside* the door, when I go out and lock up."

I pulled out my wallet and extracted my driving license, with a key tucked inside it. "About once a month I have to use it."

I slid a business card from my wallet and handed it to Tory, "Ask your hosts if I live anywhere near where they live. I would love to see you while you are on holiday in Winnipeg,"

I climbed off my knees and stood up to let a passenger heading for the washroom go past. "I'll look for you in the arrivals area; you know, where we collect our luggage." They nodded and I headed back to my seat farther forward in the airplane.

But it didn't work out that way; not at all.

I waited by the luggage carousel until all the passengers were off and there were no pieces of luggage still circling round and round, then walked over to the Air Canada desk and enquired about two children dressed in school uniforms.

"Oh, they were first off the plane," the clerk said. "Special arrangement, to get them to their hotel."

I asked if he knew where, which hotel.

"No idea. The passenger agent whisked them away. She was in a hurry to get home, for her Christmas dinner."

When I checked in at the Delta Hotel fifteen minutes later, I enquired if they were by some chance registered there.

"No. No one like that. Sorry."

And there my Christmas 'adventure' with Tory and Jasmyn seemed to have drifted to an unsatisfactory conclusion. I felt immensely sad for them, but could do nothing more to relieve the misery of their lonely evening..

~~~

My Christmas, however, continued the very next day. The family greeted me at Winnipeg airport and whisked me away for another round of Christmas Celebrations, and another complete Christmas Dinner. (Well, another for them, but my first!)

Instead of eight days in Winnipeg, now I had only three, for on December 29th I was booked to fly to Edmonton where I would celebrate New Year's with my son Ian and members of his family – a tradition each year.

On the 27th I was doing laundry and deciding what to pack when I had a telephone call from friends who live in Elie, some 35 kilometres west of Winnipeg. "We're driving into the city tomorrow and would like to see you before the Season is over."

"Sure," I said. "That would be great. Will you have time for lunch? Or supper?"

"Lunch would be fine. Thanks."

We settled on 12:30 and I started making a mental list of groceries I needed to buy.
~~~

I had met Ken two years earlier, when he joined the gliding club near Starbuck, where I fly, and had watched him fly his first solo in mid-summer and achieve his Transport Canada pilot's licence before the end of the season. I had also met his wife Maureen at an end-of-summer social in the clubhouse and had enjoyed their company.

On Wednesday, I had just set a plate of cold cuts, three kinds of bread, assorted salad items and my still-untouched Christmas cake on the dining table, when the doorbell rang. A glance at my kitchen clock showed it was 12:28.

I had assumed that just Ken and Maureen would be visiting, but through the peep-hole in my front door I could see what seemed to be a crowd on my doorstep.

As I pulled open the door, Maureen said: "I hope it's all right, but we have brought the twins with us and a couple of their friends." She and Ken stepped to one side and immediately I heard another voice: "Yes, yes! It *is* him!"

Ken and Maureen's twin boys pushed a grinning Tory and Jasmyn toward me. The latter immediately leapt through the door and gave me a bear-like hug.

"Christmas was just wonderful!" she breathed into my shoulder.

"It was brilliant!" Tory stepped through the door and shook my hand. "We couldn't say goodbye because they whisked us off the airplane before anyone else, and as soon as we had cleared customs they put us in a taxi and drove us to a motel in Calgary."

"So you didn't get to Winnipeg on Christmas Day?"

"We didn't need to!" That was Jasmyn, who was shrugging off her coat. "Christmas came to us!"

Gradually, as they munched on sandwiches, the story came out, a bit higgledy-piggledy as both Jasmyn and Tory—and their young friends—excitedly traced the events leading up to their special Christmas.

When, shortly after mid-day on December 23rd, Ken and Maureen heard from Tory and Jasmyn's parents that their children would be flying into Calgary on the afternoon of Christmas Day, and that they wouldn't fly on to Winnipeg until the next day, they made a fast decision. They instructed their 12-year-old twin sons to strip the decorations from the Christmas tree and pack them in a box; they packed the turkey, Christmas cake, and all the table trimmings into their SUV; and they told the boys to stuff clothing for two days into their backpacks. Early the following morning they started driving west, planning to be in Calgary by late evening. They had already booked rooms in a motel near the Calgary airport and arranged to rent the party lounge and to have access to the kitchen so they could cook their turkey. They even stopped on the outskirts of Calgary to find a stall that was still selling Christmas trees.

So when, the following afternoon, Tory and Jasmyn pushed open the door to what they had been told would be their room, instead of seeing a scantily furnished anonymous motel bedroom, they were greeted by the smell of roasting turkey, the sight of decorations on the walls and balloons bouncing against the ceiling, a decorated Christmas tree in the corner, and joyous shouts of "Merry Christmas! Merry Christmas!" Suddenly, they realized, they were going to be *with* the family they had really wanted to spend their Christmas.

"O-o-h," Jasmyn purred, her eyes glistening with her memory of the excitement, "it was the best Christmas ever! EVER!"

"And just when we were expecting to have no Christmas at all," Tory concurred (his eyes, too, were bright). "I couldn't believe that anyone would drive that far just so we could be with them for Christmas."

He told me later that the drive back to Winnipeg, on Boxing Day, had really opened his eyes to the distances between cities in Canada. "Sixteen hours! But I don't think Jasmyn really noticed, because she slept most of the way!"

Later, Tory and I worked out why I hadn't cottoned-on to the connection between them and Ken and Maureen and their twins.

"That was my fault," Tory was quick to assert, turning the pages of his diary. "I thought the address said *close to* Portage" (which *I* had assumed meant Portage Avenue in Winnipeg), "but it really says *on the way to* Portage" (which I now realized meant Portage la Prairie, a town 90 kilometres west of Winnipeg).

It was much later in the afternoon—in fact, early evening and already dark—before my six friends slipped on their parkas and snow boots, and tramped out through the snow to Ken's SUV. I stood at my door for a long time after they left, watching the snow drifting down and thinking that Ken and Maureen had acted in the true spirit of Christmas to ensure that Tory and Jasmyn *did* have the Christmas they had so anticipated.

It was another six months later, in the summer out at the gliding club, before I learned from Ken how they had come to know Tory and Jasmyn.

"Seven years ago the company I work for transferred me to England and we rented a house just across the road from the Haywarden's," he explained. Then he laughed: "Maureen and I really loved being there, and so did the boys, except for all that rain!"

"And though Maureen didn't push it," he added, "I knew she was awfully homesick. So after five years I asked to be transferred back to Canada."

~~~

And of course there is a postscript: In my laptop I recently opened up an email from Tory and Jasmyn, in which they have invited me to spend Christmas with them, and so meet their parents in Warwick. I think you can imagine that it was Jasmyn who emailed me: “You have just *got* to come! Christmas won’t be right without having you here with us. And it won’t be in a lonely hotel! Promise, please. Please!”

And Tory inserted a postscript: “Mother and Father insisted *they* should be sending the invitation, but we said—and eventually they agreed—that you would be more likely to come if the invitation were to come from Jas and me.”

Then Jasmyn couldn’t resist adding another note: “There will be no ice-storm to prevent you coming next year. That’s a promise!”

So I inserted a new entry in my calendar: *Fly to Heathrow December 23rd.* At first I added: *Take National Express coach to Warwick.* But since then I have happily erased it, since Tory has emailed that they and their parents would drive to Heathrow and meet me.

To be *met* at Heathrow: well, for me, that will be a first!
~~~

Oxford
Guernsey
Auckland
Mexico

7

A Christmas I Would Like

Because I have travelled fairly extensively over the years—and continue to do so—I have frequently been asked where I would most like to spend Christmas, if I had such a choice.

Now, that *is* a difficult question, because I am perfectly happy with the routine I am accustomed to.

If I really had to make such a decision, I would choose Guernsey for the early part of Christmas Eve. I would love to replicate the experience of my youth, described at the end of Chapter 3, by strolling from beside the Press Shop on Smith Street, down the hill to the junction of High Street and the Pollett, then turning to the right, down the still-cobbled length of High Street, and again turning right into the Commercial Arcade.

Sadly, however, both Le Cheminant's Toy Shop and Le Noury's Tea Shop are no longer there, so I cannot repeat those experiences. But I can walk out on to Victoria Pier, climb up onto the harbour wall, and watch the lights from Castle Cornet reflected in the water among the hulls of fishing boats rising gently up and down in the swell of the incoming tide.

For late evening I would like to be in Oxford, to attend midnight mass in St. Mary's Church on 'The High,' which is the name used locally for the High Street which curves in a gentle arc from the River Cherwell to the city centre, known as Carfax.

I would remember how, after the Service my wife Irene and I, accompanied by Irene's Aunt Dorothy and Uncle Jack, would be invited by the rector of St. Mary's to join him and his family in their home behind the church. There we would enjoy hot mulled wine and mince pies straight from the oven, before walking home through the dark roads, feeling the cool but easy atmosphere that reflected how Oxford was then.

Who would I like to be with on Christmas Day, if for once I happen not to be with my own family? There are many, many choices, each exerting a significant pull, each equally appealing in its own particular way.

Probably, if I could wind back the clock, it would be to spend the day with the three 'lions' in Auckland, New Zealand: Hannah, Michael, and Isabella. And of course their parents Phillip and Willa, who have treated me to a warm, spontaneous afternoon and evening in their home on each of my previous visits.

And then I would travel to the South Island for New Year's Eve, to the lovely city of Christchurch, where I would revisit a bed and breakfast within a few paces of the art gallery and renew my acquaintance with Sam and Hannah (another Hannah) and their parents Des and Tracey. You will have met Hannah in Auckland and Sam in Christchurch in Chapter 3, who both contributed letters about the way they observe Christmas.

But there is an even more compelling and more recent destination: I would love to go back to Warwick, in England, to revisit Torrance and Jasmyn (from Chapter 6) and their parents, for another Christmas *not* aboard an airliner.

Whichever choice I make will undoubtedly become a significant part of a future Christmas letter, and perhaps appear in a second edition of this book.

About the Author

Ron Blicq has had an adventurous career: he flew as a navigator for 15 years with the Canadian Air Force and the Royal Air Force in the UK (currently he flies with the Winnipeg Gliding Club, piloting engine-less aircraft), he has been a technical editor with CAE Industries in Winnipeg, and a teacher of technical communication with Red River College. He has authored six textbooks on writing well, three novels, and many plays. (For books written for youthful readers, he writes under the pseudonym *Veronica Steele.*)

Although supposedly "retired," he continues to teach writing workshops for Canadian and UK businesses, is very active as a playwright and director, and has won numerous awards for his works. These include the Samuel French 2008 award for best Canadian play *(Closure)* and the Guernsey Amateur Dramatic and Operatic Club best playwright and new director awards for his play *Sudoku Fever* (2009). Blicq lives in Winnipeg, Canada, but travels frequently to Guernsey, the island of his birth, in the UK.

ACKNOWLEDGMENTS

My sincere thanks to the Friesen Press team who guided me through the production process for The Spirit of Giving, and particularly my production coordinator Carmen Sum, book designer Jordan Mitchell, and illustrator Kelly Ulrich. Also to Peter Reimold, for providing additional photographs for Chapter 5.

And a third vote of thanks to Robert Hayes and Holly Steele, both in Winnipeg, who consistently monitor my progress and the suitability of the words I write.